EXPEDITION

THE MARTIAN LOGS

SAMANTHA MEEK

1.
THE ARRIVAL
Earth. 2053A.D///Mars. 1A.C

THE NEXT TIME that Captain John Morgan's feet would touch solid ground, he'd be on another planet. Was the thought scary? Terrifying, if truth be told, though he wouldn't admit it. So many journalists had asked him for his opinions on the mission, and he hadn't told any of them that he was scared. That the thought of never coming home was hard to process.

Space wasn't as bad as he thought it would be. Actually, it was rather peaceful. By now the sound of rattling, the occasional jolt of the engines and the feeling of weightlessness was relaxing, normal. Seven months can do that to a man. He'd lost six stone on this spacecraft, spending his days floating about the rocket and taking care of his crew. He'd be missing his weight when they landed, and he'd have to stand on his own two feet again. The closer Landing Day got, the more nervous about walking he became.

"We're nearly ready, Captain," Nate reported when John pulled himself through the small opening into the cockpit. Nate was strapped into his seat, pressing buttons on the screen and panels around him. At each tap of a button, John heard parts of the spacecraft coming to life, preparing for the landing manoeuvres.

"How's it looking down there?"

"Why not go up and take a look? See if you can drag Cassie away from the view," Nate joked, pausing to shoot a look at John. Unlike the Captain, Nate was still a young man, quick to laugh and joke, though sometimes the crew wished he wouldn't. John sighed.

"How often—"

"Whenever she can," Nate replied easily, eyes turning back to the panels. "We should be set for a smooth descent, a few miles out from the land site if the wind is merciful."

"Try and get as close as you can, Nate, I don't think any of us are up for a long walk."

Nate snorted and John let him work, using small ropes and handholds to pull himself along and out of the room, turning what could've been upward, but without anything pulling him down his sense of direction had become confused. It had been an incredibly disorientating experience at first, trying to get used to the feeling of weightlessness. John had always known what gravity felt like, and so living without it left him in a spin; literally. Learning how to wash, eat, sleep, and move when constantly floating in the air was a novelty at first. The crew had their fun in the beginning, laughing as Nate would find the heaviest object in the vessel that wasn't fixed in place and pretend to lift it effortlessly. But by now, they were either fed up with the sensation, as Lucia was, or so used to it that they functioned on auto pilot. John would occasionally surprise himself with how well he'd adapted to zero-gravity, and he worried about what would happen when they reached Mars.

There was only one forward-facing window on the whole of Calista II; during take-off, the force was so great that most of the hull of the craft was reinforced with thick metal and heat-proof sheets for protection, but a single porthole had been placed on the top floor. For the last few months, it had been quiet in that small viewing area; the crew had been more interested in the rear view, watching Earth get smaller and smaller as they left it behind. Once Earth was out of sight, attention shifted to the other windows, tiny but offering a small view of the endless expanse of space, stars and asteroids and empty blackness. Now Mars was fully in view, now the Calista was all but orbiting, the front window was getting more attention.

"If that glass wasn't thicker than my torso I'd be worried you'll fall through it."

Cassie startled, letting go of the small handle beside the window, drifting upward.

"Don't scare me like that," she huffed, wind-milling her arms in an attempt to reach it again, to no avail. "Dammit."

"Nate tells me you're up here a lot."

"Nate tells everyone a lot of things," Cassie replied, finally managing to get hold of the handle again and pull herself toward the window. John made his way over to get a look. He was often too busy with managing the others to really stop and admire the view. He gazed out over the front of the Calista II, and saw Mars in all its glory; the light was shining on the red planet, and though John knew that it was smaller than Earth, it looked massive up close. In all his life, he'd never seen something so awe-inspiring, something that not many people got to see in person.

"I didn't think about it until now," Cassie said quietly.

"Think about what?" He asked.

"The arrival. Stepping foot on Mars. Part of me has gotten used to floating up here."

"You'll feel differently once we've landed," John promised. "You'll get to set up your greenhouse, like you wanted."

John always felt his age when he spoke to Cassandra Kane; she was barely twenty five, and he knew she felt cooped up on the ship, a little lost; it was hard to do her job of growing plant life when plants preferred to grow on the ground. Hopefully, she'd perk up once they were back on their feet. Hopefully they all would.

"Captain, we're getting a message through Hera; looks like our girl is working well. NASA is joining the Agency to talk us through landing."

John's comms collar had been buzzing less and less as they got closer to Hera; the satellite was made for communicating with

Earth from Mars, and now they were well in her space the quality of his comms unit had increased tenfold. Nate may well have been speaking in his ear, it was so clear.
"Great, I'll get the crew into landing positions. Cassie, are you ready to see our new home from the ground?"
Cassie turned away from the window, and nodded.
"Yes Captain. I'll grab Tabitha- she never wears her comms unit when working."

John sent out the announcement over comms; that after seven long months of space travel, the crew of the Calista II were finally ready to land on Mars. They wouldn't get the glory of being the very first humans there- Japan had taken that title- but the UK had sent them off with a bang, so proud that their country would have a colony on another planet. John sighed as he re-entered the cockpit and secured himself to his seat. It hardly mattered which country had colonies where. This was their chance of survival, and as expected the media had turned it into a competition. They'd actually dubbed it 'SPACE RACE; PART II'. Anthony had found that funny, but John couldn't quite see the humour in pitting countries against each other when so many of them were already at war.

One by one, the rest of the crew appeared. Lucia and Sebastian had some sort of run in at the door, shoving each other jokingly as they squeezed through and into their seats. Anthony came after, nearly taking Nate's head off when he mis-calculated the force of his entry and entered the now crowded space feet first.

"Do you want us to crash?" Nate cried, only half serious.

"If it will get me on solid ground I'll jump out now," Anthony replied. Lucia rolled her eyes.

"Just sit down, you clumsy bastard. Where's Cassie and Tabitha?"

"Tab takes her comms out when she works, it interferes with the equipment," Anthony shrugged.

"Cassie is fetching her," John said, and the crew nodded, satisfied.

When the women arrived and were seated, Nate put Calista II into landing mode. The UK space agency had spent months collaborating with NASA and other space programmes to perfect their space craft, ensuring that this rocket won't malfunction like the original Calista. John had to admit, he was a little nervous about the landing, especially since the rocket was named after one that had crashed and burned during a test flight, but he had to have faith in those on the ground and trust that they worked out all the kinks.

If not, he could die knowing he'd be remembered as part of the first group of people to die on Mars. It was a record at least, wasn't it?

Nate began flipping switches at an alarming rate, Tabitha assisting as a co-pilot. Most rockets of the last few years had been experimenting with manual operation, and Calista II was no different. The Agency and NASA still had some control, but for the most part, Nate was the one keeping the rocket steady.

“Brace yourselves, we’re entering the atmosphere,” he announced, and the craft shuddered, John feeling a jolt in his gut that made him tense. The sudden force was intense, the crew now feeling a gravitational pull for the first time in seven months. John wondered how he’d been able to cope with it for nearly 50 years. It was… uncomfortable, to say the least.

“Anthony has passed out,” Lucia shouted over the sound of groaning metal and a loud rumbling noise that could’ve been wind or yelling. John’s ears had popped.

“Lucky bastard!” Cassie yelled back. John thought he might get bruises from how forcefully he was being tossed around in his seat, very grateful for the straps which kept him from being thrown against the walls.

“We’re not slowing down enough,” Nate was saying into his comms unit. “We need to start the thrusters. What do you mean, no?! Well I’m using the parachute now. We’re going too fast.”

The feeling of being slowed down suddenly had John nearly throwing up his last meal. The crew all made noises of complaint, Anthony coming to with a yell.

“Oh God,” he whined. “Let me pass out again. It was so much easier being unconscious.”

“Shut up,” Tabitha ordered. “Nate, we’ve only got a few minutes, what’s the issue with the gear?”

“NASA is saying that the jets aren’t all running at full power. Programming issue.”

"Which means?"

"If we start using them, it could send us into a spin, or completely blow us off course."

"Can we manually re-programme them?" Tabitha asked.

"If we're given access."

"Nate, tell whoever you're speaking to, to give us access. Tabitha, see what you can do." John ordered.

Tabitha nodded and turned to a small console where code was appearing on screen. The Agency had recruited only the best for their pioneer mission to Mars, and Tabitha fit that description to a T; she'd been part of the team on the ground originally, hired to build the Calista and all her equipment, but eventually the Agency knew that there was no one better to send to their new colony as an engineer. Looking at how swiftly she was locating the thruster's programming issue, they weren't wrong about her.

"Don't wanna rush you Tab, but we only have six minutes from atmosphere to solid ground, and we're already over halfway down," Nate said.

"Not to worry; it was just a small error. Turn them on."

"You're sure?" John asked.

"Yes. Turn them on."

John felt better at the sound of powerful jets turning themselves on and slowing the rocket speed. The Rovers and other equipment they had sent ahead had all been fitted with cushioning and bounced on landing, but the Calista had human cargo, and so they had to try and land as smoothly as possible; any bouncing could damage the ship and them. It was a shaky descent, still a little on the fast side, according to Nate, but not too fast that they would die on impact. Little victories.

"The lower camera is on," Tabitha reported. "There's a few rocks, but at this speed I don't think hitting them will damage us too badly."

"As long as they don't breach the ship, we're okay," John agreed. "This craft won't be flying again, a few dents won't matter as long as we can still occupy her whilst we build the base."

"We're in a good position, the ground is flat- everyone brace yourselves for landing."

John held his breath. His wife always used to laugh at him for it, a simple reflex he couldn't help. He missed her still. Imagining her laughing helped him stay calm as Calista made contact with Mars, not too lightly. Without that seatbelt, John was certain his head would've collided with the ceiling.

"We've landed successfully," Nate reported. "The Calista II and its crew are now citizens of Mars."

"Hallelujah," Sebastian sighed. "How's Anthony doing?"

"I think he's passed out again," Lucia replied, not sounding too sympathetic.

"Nate, Tabitha, good job- turn on all outer cameras, let's get a look at where we are and we'll send out Explorer."

"Yes Sir."

The small screens at the front of the cockpit began displaying pictures instead of code and graphs. Calista II was fitted with several outer cameras, positioned so that they had a 360 degree view of their surroundings.

"We're in a crater," Lucia said flatly. John leaned forward. He expected to see a few rocks, red sand, and miles and miles of empty land. Instead, there were high ridges surrounding the craft a few miles away, with no sign of decline.

"We can't be," Nate frowned. "Of course we're not—"

Nate rotated the cameras.

"Mission control are using Hera to look for us. We're definitely in a crater," Tabitha confirmed.

"Jesus," Sebastian huffed. "What does that mean for us?"

"Let me see," John instructed, and Tabitha carefully climbed out of her seat to let him take over, seeing each view from Calista II up close. The impact crater was deep, looking at the size of the surrounding ridges, and would protect them from the worst of the Martian winds. The land inside was less cluttered than what he expected, with less large rocks and uneven terrain. Whatever had made this crater had been broken up on impact, and only pieces remained.

"It means," John announced, turning to look at his crew. "You're looking at the future New Kingdom base site. Welcome to your new home, everyone. Let's get to work."

2.
THE NEW KINGDOM COLONY
EARTH 2053///MARS 1A.C

SEBASTIAN WAS NOT a fan of enclosed spaces. He never had been. Setting up a colony on a brand-new planet seemed like a great idea at first thought, as he had imagined they'd be placed in a wide-open area with plenty of space to move around in. Seeing the view from Calista's cameras had unnerved him.

Three weeks into the colonization mission, and he was still feeling a little caged in.

"You look like you're having a caffeine withdrawal," Lucia joked, joining him in their central hub one morning. So far, the base was only partially set up; they had a few rooms for sleeping, eating and building, a small space where Cassie would start her hydroponic farming, and an airlock seal to the outside. Anthony was constantly out there, doing god-knows-what. Sebastian supposed that as he was a geologist, the outside must be more interesting to him than inside.

"Not quite used to that extra thirty minutes," Sebastian replied jokingly.

"Do we still call them minutes? This whole 'Martian calendar' is confusing as hell."

"Minutes, seconds and hours are all the same," Sebastian told her.

"Thank God. What are you doing in here, anyway? Didn't Captain ask you to start working with Explorer today?"

Lucia rolled her eyes.

"Tabitha has kidnapped him," she replied. "It's only to be expected, she gets along better with robots than people. I've been reassigned; you've got yourself an assistant for the day."

Sebastian's job was an odd one, especially whilst the base was in the midst of being built. He was supposed to be the Chief Physicist, he and Lucia studying the magnetic field and the atmosphere of Mars. However, the base needed an architect, and John had assigned the design of their new home to Sebastian. Sebastian would oversee the completion of New Kingdom before he could get on with what he was here for.

Lucia had been Sebastian's closest friend on the Calista, and the pair spent the day in good spirits, inspecting the material and construction Rovers, designing new buildings and working through issues with construction.

"When will the next rocket arrive?" Lucia asked curiously, stood beside one of the larger crane Rovers, which was just taller than she was and far wider. It was beeping in error, and she picked a few stones from its crane. The Rover tested the extension on the crane, deemed itself fixed, and moved along. Sebastian shrugged, checking the screen on his wrist. The space suit was big, clunky, and a little obstructive, but it kept them alive when they stepped outside, so Sebastian supposed he could deal with the inconvenience.

"Cap says we will send a message through Hera when the base is built and the Agency will send the next ship."

"It'll be nice to have some more faces around here," Lucia mused, gesturing to the huge empty red space around them.

"Am I not company enough for you?" Sebastian joked.

"Oh Honey, you're the only one here who doesn't make me want to slam my head against a wall within ten minutes of conversation."

Sebastian liked the outside. As deserted as it was, it wasn't as closed in as inside the base. England had gone for a dome shape in most of its designs; rooms were all circular, connected by short corridors. Everything was air locked and the change in gravity and their strength after months in space had made things far more difficult then they would've been on earth. Cassie had struggled to open the doors on several occasions, prompting the Captain to begin daily workouts, hoping to build up the crew's muscle mass and get them used to using their strength again. Sebastian had hidden his struggle with the doors, and found that stepping outside and walking without seeing white walls lessened his feelings of claustrophobia.

"It's weird, isn't it? A yellow sky?" Lucia asked, coming to stand beside him.

"It's like the whole world is on fire," Sebastian replied quietly. The Comms in their suits allowed them to listen to each other, but it also gave the others an ear into the conversation. Sebastian didn't want Nate hearing everything he said.

"The best part about being here is the sky. You can see so many stars on a clear night."

"We're not supposed to be out at night."

"I know," Lucia sighed. "But I've always had a love of stargazing. I told the Captain I wouldn't give it up just because we're here."

The Rovers had a remote operator that lived inside the base near the Captain's space, but they could also be re-programmed manually. Sebastian caught up to the crane Rovers and punched in a few new orders on their small command screens, and off they went, ready to put together a new dome. They'll need plenty of them to have enough farming space. Sebastian frowned. It didn't seem right.

"Lucia," he called, "Can I get a second opinion?"

"You may."

"This crater seems even around the top, doesn't it?"

Lucia turned slowly on the spot, scanning the rise of the crater edges that surrounded them. They were high and steep, but according to Anthony, not massively wide, and quite level at their peak.

"It does, I suppose."

"So why would we build all of these small domes that take up so much precious space, when we could simply seal the top of the crater?"

"An ice shield would protect us from radiation," Lucia muttered. "But that would take a whole lot of ice. A lot of power. Too much time."

"We have time," Sebastian replied easily.

"But how would we get out? Nathaniel is determined to set up Rover routes between us and Tokyo, if you seal the top—"

"Anthony thinks that these walls can be dug through. We make a tunnel out, have it air locked, and we're pretty much safe to live freely under the ice."

Sebastian could imagine it; all of the oxygen they were filtering into the base so they could breathe, all of the vents feeding C02 to the plants to take in, it could all be done in the crater. No need for space suits, no need for domes or small spaces. He just had to find a way to make it work. And he had to get the Captain on board.

There was no time like the present; the moment that he and Lucia called it a day, Sebastian gathered the crew for the sol-down meal. Cassie still had dirt under her fingernails, there was a smear of oil on Tabitha's cheek, and the whole team seemed exhausted from a long day of work. They prepared their meals- potatoes, mushrooms a few nuts- and sat down together.

"I have an idea for the base," Sebastian announced. The others looked up at him curiously.

"Tell us," John replied.

And Sebastian did. As he talked, he saw doubt on a few faces, but the way that Anthony lit up gave him some confidence. At least someone would be on his side. John, as always, was much harder to read, watching Sebastian with a perfect poker face. When he was done, he waited for the Captain's thoughts.

"That's a massive project, Sebastian," he rumbled, putting down his utensils and looking Sebastian in the eye.

"I know, but it could help us make the best of what we have."

"I like the idea," Anthony said. "Tunnelling out of the crater would be great for transport and my studies. Plus the Martian sand is good for construction, and we don't have unlimited resources in here. I'm all for tunnelling out of here. We could have multiple openings on different sides—"

"Let's not get ahead of ourselves," Tabitha cut in, raising an eyebrow. "An ice roof needs support. How are you going to make sure it wouldn't collapse inward?"

"That's where I'm hoping to get your input," Sebastian replied. "The Iranians have already started mining iron from the surface, they're certain there will be stronger material further below the rock. We could build support beams."

"It's possible," Anthony allowed. "But we didn't come here to be miners. We're a farming base."

"The ice roof would free up a lot of space," Cassie sighed. "I could rig larger areas for hydroponics, it might be easier to pollinate and harvest. If the ice lets in enough light, that could also be beneficial-

-”

“It will take years,” John stated. “We need to get this base up and running ready for the next stage of colonisation. Sebastian, it’s an ambitious idea. But I’m not certain that it’s an idea for today.”

Sebastian didn’t want to admit that the Captain was right, but maybe an ice ceiling was a little too much for the situation at present. He agreed to pause any plans on it until they were set up and focus on the completion of New Kingdom, but he was glad it wasn’t completely vetoed. Now, at least, he had something to plan ahead for. Something, in a strange way, to look forward to. He knew that Lucia wouldn’t want to sacrifice her stargazing, and Nate wouldn’t be happy about the drones having no landing base within the crater, but he could see the benefits far outweighing the sacrifice. Maybe icing up the world above would help Sebastian come to terms with being on a new planet; he wouldn’t be reminded of how far from home he was every time he looked up at an unfamiliar sky.

Lucia got her turn with Explorer the next morning, and Sebastian was left to work alone. He ordered the construction Rovers around, watching as they put together another farming dome. One Rover laid a solid floor sheet, securing it to the ground over yesterday’s foundations. Two crane Rovers pieced together the plexi-glass dome bit by bit, whilst a Rover with a welding arm attached sealed any gaps tightly. Sebastian took a short walk around the perimeter of the base; from the outside it looked smaller, the domes didn't seem so high or wide, the corridors looked incredibly narrow. He tried to map out the rooms as he went; the inner-most room was the command centre, and it connected all their different needs, like a beating heart that they passed through to get to work. Tabitha worked in the Western room, where any engineering projects and repairs were carried out. Malfunctioning Rovers, faulty equipment or damaged suits were all taken to her in her sector. South of Engineering was where Anthony spent his days studying rocks and running tests on the Martian soil and sand. Cassie's farm lay East of the base, a large dome that had been filled with what water they had, a combustion chamber nearby creating more, drop by drop for them to drink. It was a slow process, trying to chemically manufacture water, but it was the only way they could get hold of it on a dry planet such as this.

Sebastian came full circle around the base, stopping where he'd left the Rovers to work. It was so quiet here; when the comms went silent, he could hear the world around him through his helmet, and it was a world away from what he'd come from. On Earth, there were no empty places. Everywhere was loud with cars and people, machine hum was a constant background noise. Sebastian hadn't realised how very loud it had been until the buzzing and whirring stopped. He wondered if eventually he would miss it. Nate already did, he knew that. The man had spent his life around loud engines, it must be unnerving to live here in the quiet.

But for now, the silence was a novelty. The clean air, though made in a combustion chamber, was refreshing. Sebastian remembered the taste of the air on Earth. It had been so thick that all year-round people in his home town wore scarves and masks around their mouths, and Doctor's offices were packed with coughing patients. Though the sky was supposed to be blue, most of the time it was hidden with thick cloud or smog, which was partly why Sebastian found Mars so strange. Yes, the air was sometimes filled with dust, but most of the time he could see for miles, right to the high walls of the crater edge. The colour of the sky, a butterscotch yellow, hadn't quite struck the right chord with him. On Earth, that was usually a sign of danger. He missed those rare blue days. Maybe he should take Lucia up on her offer of stargazing. He'd never seen a Martian sunset- and according to her, it was so blue that it felt almost like home again.

The Rovers beeped to announce that they had completed his tasks, and Sebastian turned to them again, Mars' construction crew. One day, there would be more people here to help him. He just had to get things ready for them first. Sebastian inspected the new dome, testing the air locks and pressure inside, before pressing the comms button on his collar.

"Hey Cassie, I hear you've been wanting a new space for an orchard. Would you like to come and approve the dome?"

3.
THE WELCOMING
EARTH 2054/// MARS 1 A.C

NATE WAS SO READY for this. He'd been ready for the last several months. When Sebastian had finally announced that the base was ready for more people, Nate had been the one to run to the Captain to tell him. Sebastian was still annoyed about it, but Nate couldn't care less; the thought of having more people around made everything better.

"Nathaniel," the Captain said, once everyone was gathered in the command centre. "They won't be landing in the crater. How close could you guide them to us?"

"I'll drop them right at our front door, Sir," Nate replied easily, cracking his knuckles. Sebastian rolled his eyes. Something about Sebastian hadn't sat right with Nate from the beginning; he was too quiet, too deadpan. Everything Nate said, Sebastian did the opposite. Everything Sebastian wanted, Nate hated.

"They're coming into orbit, they'll need a few hours to get into position. Be ready for them, Nathaniel. They need you on comms in case a remote landing is necessary. Anthony, is the tunnel completely ready and secure?"

"Yes Sir," Anthony confirmed. "I used it again this morning.

Lucia was right; Martian concrete is just as good as Earth's. Better, even. Needs less water. For the next tunnel I would suggest borrowing Washington's printer though, I think a stronger drill might—"

"A simple yes would've been fine, Anthony," the Captain sighed, as he had so many times before. Nate snorted. Poor Anthony, just a simple man who spent all day surrounded by rocks; no wonder he talked a mile a minute when he had the chance.

"Right. Sorry, Sir."

"Lucia, Sebastian, any thoughts?"

"It all looks good from here, Sir," Lucia reported, sitting in front of a screen, looking at the data that the colony ship Beginnings was sending them about its position above the Martian atmosphere. It was circling a little too low for Nate's liking, but Lucia knew her stuff; if she was confident that everything was fine, he found it better not to worry himself too much.

"They're orbiting pretty close," Sebastian commented, leaning over Lucia's shoulder. "Keep an eye on that, Nate."

"I've got it," Nate hissed in response.

"I'm just saying—"

"It's the way you said it."

"And how did I say it?"

Nate turned to glare at the older man. Everyone had aged on Mars, but not Sebastian; his dark skin showed no wrinkles or lines from tiredness, his eyes were alert and intelligent. Nate didn't trust people who didn't show weakness.

"Let's not do this now," the Captain growled. "We've got people in the air to look after. Deal with your issues once they're safe inside our walls."

Tabitha was rolling her eyes at them, standing by in case of emergency. The only two who weren't needed for the landing were Anthony and Cassie, who stood together, just out of the way of the Captain and his nervous pacing. Cassie had paled drastically in the last several months. Nate took a mental note to check on her later.

When Beginnings neared the optimal position for landing, Nate got the Crew's attention.

"Hello Beginnings, this is Nathanial Taylor. Are you hearing me?"

"Loud and clear, Sir. This is Emily Castle. We're ready to begin landing procedure on Beginnings."

"Good, we're ready on the ground. Has mission control re-connected?"

"Yes, they're back. They're saying Deimos wandered into the way, cut off the signal for a moment."

"Then we're good to go. Ready for landing. We'll see you on the ground, Beginnings."

Nate had always wanted to fly. As a child, he'd been really into planes; every child had their obsession, but whilst most moved on from their dinosaur phase as they grew, Nate's passion for flight only grew as he learned more about it. At the age of seventeen, his

Mother had allowed him to join the RAF as a pilot. He'd then moved on to remotely operating aircraft systems. When the UK space agency had announced that they were looking for someone to pilot the Calista II to Mars, Nate had applied first, asked questions later. He still remembered his Mum's reaction; a hand to the chest, tea promptly placed on the table, and the words "do you even know how to fly a rocket?" Turns out, it was just as complex as a plane, but Nate was determined, and he made it.

He missed his Mum sometimes. Hopefully Mission control would hurry up and get on with making that Earth-Mars messaging system they'd mentioned a good year ago. He wanted to hear someone other than mission control and the people in the room around him. He wanted his Mum to say she was proud of him.

Beginnings was a shoddy comparison to Calista; it was rather like comparing a luxury tour bus belonging to a world famous mega-star to the 135 TFGM bus at peak time on a Monday. It just didn't have the grace or the manoeuvring, but it did the job. It carried 100 Brits around 86 million miles, and that was good enough. Nate brought up the controls that Emily would be working with in the air, Hera syncing the two together so he could guide them if need be. She was doing a good job; a minute into the descent, and Miss Castle was on target, albeit a little off centre. Nate adjusted the ship's spin speed, ensuring that Beginnings wouldn't start to tumble out of control. A Rover landing was full of bumps and bouncing, but it was imperative that this rocket make it to the ground upright and without rolling.

"How are you doing?" Nate asked, three minutes into the fall.

"I think some of the passengers have fainted," Emily reported. Tabitha giggled.

"Happens to the best of us," Nate told her. "You'll need to be powering up the jets, slow down time starts now. You are a little heavier than we were, get those propulsion rockets ready now."

"Yes Sir."

The crew on the ground were tense. Nate could feel it. He could feel the eyes of those not doing anything burning into his back as he tweaked controls, straightening the rocket and helping her slow down. He wished they'd stop staring. Surely they had better things to do than to breathe down his neck.

"How far out will we end up, Nathaniel? We have space suits, but we've been in space too long to make it too far."

"Worry not, Washington gifted us their newest Rovers for a sol or two to get you into the base; each one carries five people including a driver, but I can pilot it from here too. You'll only be a few miles out. Lucia, if I send you the predicted co-ordinates, can you send out the Rovers? All six, if you would."

Nate plotted Beginning's landing area on the map and sent the coordinates to Lucia's screen. He heard Rovers waking up from outside a few seconds later. Washington's transport Rovers were much bigger than a family car, with large wheels and a cargo space that could fit around three Martian weeks of supplies in it. The sound they made when the engines were on made Nate feel like he was back in an Earth city again.

"Brace yourselves," Nate announced. He couldn't see Beginnings on screen, but he could see its 'dashboard'; its data, levels of oxygen, heat signature and distance from the ground. When the distance hit 0m, he panicked.

"Emily? Beginnings, can you read me?"

"Nathaniel, what's wrong?" the Captain demanded.

"The cockpit is situated at the very top of the ship."

"And?"

"It has a distancing meter. If it's at 0—"

"Then the top of the ship is touching the Martian surface," Lucia said, realisation dawning on her face suddenly.

"Oh no," Cassie whispered.

"Beginnings, please respond," Nate tried again. The silence on the other end of his comms made him feel cold. There were 100 people on that ship. He opened another channel of communication, sending a request to Mission Control through Hera.

"We're reading you," a voice said when the signal went through.

"This is Nathanial Taylor, of New Kingdom. Do you have contact with Beginnings?"

"Our comms have disconnected. What is their condition?"

"They're not responding Sir. It looks like the ship has landed on its side."

The beat of silence on the other end didn't make Nate feel any better. He heard his own heartbeat in that second of hesitation.

"We are able to turn on Beginning's outer cameras. We will send you the images."

Nate knew it was John who was leaning over his shoulder, the rest of the team crowding behind him to look. Most of the cameras were showing similar images of red sand, some images completely black. The camera that had been attached to the cockpit was capturing pictures of the Martian sky. *That shade of yellow is so depressing*, Nate thought to himself.

"Dammit," John muttered. "Nate, try them again."

"Yes, Sir. Beginnings, are you reading us? Beginnings, please respond."

There was a cackling sound, like static, but Nate thought he heard the sound of breathing, a distorted voice trying to reply. The team seemed to sigh all at once.

"Don't get too happy," John snapped. "They could be hurt. Anthony, Sebastian, catch up with those Rovers, go and see what's happening."

Both men nodded and hurried from the room. John laid a hand on Nate's shoulder.

"Get their comms up and running, Nathanial," he ordered. "We need to be able to speak to them."

Nate didn't even need to say anything, Tabitha knew when she was needed. She nearly shoved him right off his chair, the pair both half-sitting on it whilst they worked. She was better at this sort of thing than he was, but that didn't mean he was useless; it was just very hard to be better at technology than Tabitha.

"Looks like the ship tipped on landing; there's a breach."

"Where?"

"There, one of the cargo holds. That whole thing will have blown the second there was even a pinhole in the metal, the force of it could've been what tipped the craft."

"Do you think anyone was hurt?"

"If everyone was strapped in, they all would've been far away from the hold; and each section is secured, it won't have damaged the rest of the ship. Unfortunately, that'll be a lot of supplies strewn across the ground."

"Well, luckily for us, Captain sent someone else to collect it," Nate joked. Tabitha smirked.

"That is true. Ah, I think someone on Beginnings is fixing up their comms."

The crackling became a buzz, which then faded into background hum. Nate took a breath.

"Beginnings? Can you read us?"

"We read you," Emily replied. Tabitha seemed to deflate beside him, nodding to herself.

"Thank God, are you all okay?"

"Everyone is fine; one of our holds breached and tipped us."

"We've got people coming to you, the Rovers will be there in twenty minutes. We'll have to make a few trips, so prioritise who's going first and which supplies will go with them. Emily, we're so glad you're okay."

"Me too. It would be so embarrassing to make it all the way here and die on impact."

Nate had to laugh. John didn't find it funny, and Tabitha only managed a smile, but Nate felt his spirits lift.

"Well you'd hold the record for being the first ones to die on Mars; you'd get your names on a plaque for that."

Tabitha smacked his arm, and Nate just knew that John's head had found his hands. Whatever. Emily had laughed. At least there would be someone around who found him funny, at last.

Anthony and Sebastian checked in with base when they reached the ship, and they began sending over the passengers. Nate and Cassie waited in the Command centre for the arrivals, whilst John headed for the airlock entrance and Lucia and Tabitha donned suits to greet them outside. Cassie was smiling.

"It'll be nice to have a few new faces here," she said, tapping her fingers against her legs. Nate frowned.

"Yeah. You seem nervous."

"Do I?"

"Just a tad."

"I've not spoken to anyone outside of our team for nearly a year."

"An Earth year," Nate corrected. "It's only been a few months

here."
Cassie sighed.
"You know what I mean."

Nate wanted to say more. He always did, but the issue was that there never seemed to be enough time. Building a new civilisation from scratch made it really hard to stop and have a meaningful conversation. When he turned to badger Cassie about what was bothering her, the hissing of an airlock seal stopped him. Had they travelled that fast? The first group were already here? He heard John greeting them, and voices- so many voices! It sounded busy, and Nate had almost forgotten what truly busy sounded like. The noise got louder as people approached, and he found himself getting emotional when the arrivals began filing into the Command centre. All six rovers had been filled, and the once empty room now contained thirty more people. They all looked so happy, and Nate's cheeks began to hurt already from smiling back at them.

"Welcome to Mars!"

The cheering was exhilarating; all this time it had been so quiet, he had often found himself talking in hushed tones, not wanting to disturb the peace. Now he cheered and laughed and greeted people with his outside voice and he revelled in it.

"Make yourself at home! Are any of you pilots, by any chance?"

"I am, and you better recognise me," a young man grinned. Nate let out a yelp.

"Jesus, Oscar, is that you?!"
He pulled his old RAF buddy into a hug.
"Two whole planets and I still have the misfortune of running into you!" Oscar grinned.
"Shut up, you heard I was here and had to come join me. Have you met Cassie yet?"
He introduced them, and in came the next wave of people.

Two hours after the landing, New Kingdom had grown from a population of six to one hundred and six, and Nate had never been more cheerful. This was a godsend; because not only had it been a delivery of people, but this was a group of people with skills. There were engineers, botanists, builders, pilots and scientists. It was a selection of people who would really kick-start the growth of the base. Yes, Sebastian had built the initial structure to allow the 100 people to arrive, but now they could step in and get down to business. Over dinner, Nate heard groups discussing plans to start building another farming dome, to expand the engineering spaces, to go ahead with Sebastian's Ice Ceiling; which, if Nate had anything to do with it, would not be happening. Finally, Nate remembered why he'd jumped at the chance to come to Mars, and looked forward instead of back. Earth was home, but it was dead. The people in charge had lost their way, everything was about money and power and greed. Here, money didn't exist. People were excited about their ideas without worrying about the cost. No one would be paid for their labour, but they didn't want to be;

everyone in New Kingdom was here to make something new and beautiful. Whoever these people were on Earth, they were equal on Mars. Nate looked about the packed eating hall, barely seeing a familiar face, but smiling anyway. He was looking into the future, and he saw it, bright and shining.

4.
THE TROUBLE WITH COLONIES
EARTH 2055///MARS 2A.C

IF THIS WAS LIFE ON MARS, Cassie was beginning to regret her decision to come. It wasn't like she was suffering physically; it was actually much cleaner on Mars, her personal garden grew better in manufactured conditions then it did in the ruined Earth environment. She could breathe easier, sleep a little longer. It was her mind that suffered here. She missed going outside, missed the feeling of gravity, and the privacy of living alone. Here, everyone was living on top of one another. There were nearly twenty to a sleeping quarter, the bathrooms were uncomfortable and there was always a wait time. Cassie couldn't enjoy the simple pleasure of eating in silence. Even her farming domes, once her own personal space, had been taken over by strangers. Polite strangers, but still strangers.

And if the atmosphere had been tense when there were only six people cooped up in a confined space, it was several times worse now.

"Boys!" Tabitha yelled, she and Cassie stepping into the eating hall for a mid-sol snack. Sol. Cassie still hadn't warmed to the word. She forgot that Sols and days were different, that a Martian week had eight days- sols- and not seven, that the years were nearly twice as long and crawled along three times as slowly. Not even the sight of a potential fist fight had sparked any adrenaline. She just wanted a handful of mushrooms to snack on and to get back to her garden.

"Nate! How did I know you'd be involved?!"

Cassie let her get on with it; people listened to Tabitha instinctively, it's not like she needed any help. She returned swiftly to her crops, deciding to forget the mushrooms and wait until the sol down meal.

The farming domes had doubled in the last few months; New Kingdom had welcomed in the first ever Martian New Year with a massive building project, really striving to establish themselves as Mars' official farming colony. Washington could have its ground travel, Tokyo could go ahead and be the global terraformers. Europa could churn out medical quick-fixes and NAMC could study all they ice they wanted, but they would be nothing without New Kingdom and their revolutionary farming strategies. Cassie had overseen the first shipment of potatoes to Iran, watching the fully-loaded Rover drive away through the exit tunnel. She had watched wistfully until it disappeared, and her suit beeped to let her know her oxygen tank was running low. Anthony had now set up a large room they could use to load rovers without the need for suits, but Cassie found herself missing walking on the sand, seeing the world around her, albeit through a thick visor.

The atmosphere in the newest dome was cheerful, a buzz of excitement in the air.

“Do you think the Captain would let any of us go and see it?”

“Nah, a waste of fuel just to go and look at an old robot.”

“A legendary robot,” a young man was saying, wistful. They were fixing a leaky pipe, though why it took two men to repair one pipe, Cassie didn’t know. As long as they hurried up and repaired it before too much water was wasted, she didn’t mind.

“Oh god, you’re one of the Opportunity fanboys. It’s just a robot, man.”

“She has been here for so long, waiting for us to rescue her! Washington must be so happy to have found her, apparently NASA have officially declared the day a holiday on Earth.”

“As if there aren’t bigger problems they should be worrying about,” the older man snorted. Cassie rolled her eyes, and inspected the small sprouts of green that were growing at even intervals in rows. The water would be circulated over and over again, full of the nutrients that plants needed without using soil. Cassie could see the roots on the lettuce she was trying to nurse into adulthood, though the low gravity was proving a challenge for her plants. Certain crops just wouldn’t grow. She’d quickly given up on watercress and delicate flowers, quickly germinating some of their sturdier plants like potatoes, mushrooms and fruit trees. So far, the trees were growing steadily, though whether they would produce any fruit was yet to be seen. The Martian conditions were affecting Cassie's farms in strange ways, and no one could figure out why. Lucia was running with her theory of magnetic fields, and Anthony promised Cassie he would try and see if the rock samples he collected could give her any answers, but so far it was all a mystery. Cassie just did what she could with the things that she had. Her lettuce would grow a little lopsided, the mushrooms would grow in size but not in mass, and she would have to face the questions of the hungry colonists who wanted to know why their food was looking a little odd.

When the plumbers left, Cassie checked the water supply. There just wasn't enough to feed the amount of plants she wanted to grow, since now there were more people in need of hydration. Anthony had saved the day by discovering the pockets of C02 and hydrogen that they could use to create more water, but Cassie found herself between a rock and a hard place. She needed the water to feed the people. The people needed water to stay hydrated. Not to mention the ones who demanded extra water for bathing, which irritated Cassie to no end. They needed more combustion chambers.

And all Sebastian wanted to do was build a roof. Yes, he was a smart man, with good ideas; but he wasn't great at prioritising their needs. Anthony was within reason when he hijacked a few construction rovers to drill through the crater ridge, but Sebastian needed to focus on their need for sustenance rather than better shelter. What they had worked, even if it was a little cramped and cluttered. Cassie moved away from her growing plants and toward the nursery, where she had been testing which cuttings they'd brought along would grow without problems. The onions seemed promising, but Cassie was hoping that it would be the wheat that really shone through. If she could choose anything to grow without problems, it would be wheat. So far, it was struggling, though Cassie thought she saw a small shoot sprouting from the tiny square of soil it had been planted in.

"You're doing so good," she told the plant quietly, not daring to touch it, but staring lovingly at the nursery. This was her only purpose on Mars, and she had to see it through. Absently, Cassie wished she had tried harder with the flowers; they may not be good for eating, but she felt like everything was so bare and cold without those splashes of colour.

Cassie found herself in the company of the Captain as the sol came to an end. She'd retreated into the central base when the only source of light became artificial, and bumped into her boss as he left his office space. He smiled in greeting.

"Hello Cassandra, have you had a productive day?" he asked politely.

"Most of my days are the same," she replied, trying to keep her tone light. "I only know if it's been productive when the harvest comes."

"You seem to be adjusting better as of late."

Had she? She didn't think so. Maybe she hid it better than she thought she did.

"Thank you, Captain. Did you get my request to retrieve the last of the samples from Beginnings?"

"I did, Cassie. I'm afraid it's a no, for now."

"Why?"

"None of the samples in the ship are edible." He was speaking to her like she was a child, and it was a simple matter of her wanting something trivial. She narrowed her eyes.

"Those spare supplies Lucia got aren't either, and she didn't even need them in the end."

"Cassandra—"

"It's like you think what I do is useless!"

He fixed her with a very serious look, one that he usually reserved for Nate.

"Of course I don't," he told her evenly, slowly. She rolled her eyes.

"Right, but you gave all my daily work to other people who don't have a PhD in botanical science—"

"You weren't coping with the change, Cassandra," John cut in, and she laughed, maybe a little too loudly.

"We're on another planet! We ruined Earth to the point of killing ourselves, and now we pack up and move here and none of you have learned a thing!"

"Cassandra—"

"You care more about your robots and numbers and building things that will last rather than creating a world that won't die when we get too much for it. All I wanted was a moss sample, that was it. But it's too dangerous to risk one of your precious robots, isn't it?"

He let her go when she turned to leave, shoving past the people who had gathered at the sound of shouting, uncaring of what they thought of her for it. Some cried out in anger or surprise, one tried to grab her, but Cassie just kept walking, not really sure of where she was going, but needing to go *somewhere.* She reached a door and shoved it open, following the bare white walls made of metal and human ignorance, until she met a dead end and had to find somewhere else to go. Eventually, she found herself sitting in the exit tunnel, airlock seals at either end to prevent the whole base from losing oxygen. When she would get mad on Earth, she could go outside, walk to her local park and sit on the bench, watching the trees in the wind. There were no trees here, not yet, and maybe not ever if she couldn't find a plant-worthy fix to the gravity issue. It all seemed…rather hopeless.

"That was some show of sass toward our Captain. You know, if it weren't for us all being stuck in here, maybe he would fire you."

Nate had followed her. Of course he had. And he was smiling, of all things. Cassie turned away from him.

"Bugger off," was all she said.

"Although, if he's already given your jobs to other people, he already has."

"Leave me alone, Nate."

He didn't. Instead, he sat opposite her, his long legs reaching across the space to lean against hers. She glared at him.

"You don't like Mars, do you Cass?"

"Don't call me that."

"Oh come on, don't snap at me. If you haven't noticed, I'm the only one who's come after you."

"To make fun of me," Cassie grumbled.

"Nah, not really. I thought it was good- you shouting at him. He's been getting too comfortable in charge. He didn't think about your feelings."

"Who does?" Cassie huffed. Nate snorted.

"Now you're just being bitter. Look, I'm no botanist. And I have no idea what you'd want with moss, of all things. But if it's important to you, I can put in a request to send a Rover to Beginnings. I need some spare parts for my drones anyway, and we can grab your samples whilst we're there."

"Why would you do that?" Cassie asked, looking up at him curiously. Nate had always been…hard to read. Always poking fun, sometimes too much to handle. He smiled.

"Because you're my friend, stupid. And it matters to you. Plus, I get extra parts out of it. I won't stand for Russia having cool drones when I can build and fly my own."

"Once a Pilot," Cassie muttered, but she smiled, nudging his leg with hers. "Thanks, Nate."

"Hey, no problem. And Cassie?"

"Yeah?"

"You should shout more often. People should really start hearing what you have to say."

5.
THE ICE CEILING
EARTH 2057//MARS 3A.C

IF TABITHA HEARD ONE more thing about this ice ceiling, someone would be getting friendly with her soldering iron. Buzz had been spreading about Sebastian finally asking the Captain to give the go-ahead on his plans, and that was great for him, but frankly, Tabitha could not care less. Ice ceiling or no ice ceiling, they wouldn't live any differently. The domes were built, the walls were up, and there was not enough oxygen to fill the massive inside of the crater. Compared to some other craters on Mars, New Kingdom was built in one of the smaller impact sites, but it was still too big to seal over and live in freely. They could fit five hundred more people in there and build the spaces to house them, and they would still have room to grow. Tabitha wasn't convinced they needed it.

"Miss Khan, I've finished the plans," Frank told her, coming to stand at her work table nervously. She didn't know why he was so scared of her, she'd always been nice to him. Maybe he had witnessed some of the fights she'd broken up over the years, or maybe he was just a nervous person.

"Did you include my revisions?"

"Yes ma'am."

"And specifics on diameters?"

"Yes."

"Good, hand it to Dianne and have it sent to Five."

Group Five were solely for building; they were not there for repairs, for coming up with ideas or making modifications- their one job was to build what was given to them. They were rather good at it; other people had struggled with the plans, looked at her like she'd handed them an IKEA flatpack and told them to get to work, but Five were capable of putting together even the trickiest machines with the vaguest instructions. She was fiercely protective of them, keeping them within her sector and not letting them get shipped off elsewhere.

The news that Seb was pushing for the ice ceiling made her worried about her team's future.

"Captain, please tell me that whatever is going on won't affect me," Tabitha greeted John at sol down, she and the other original crew members joining him in his office space. It was a small room where he would receive their requests on screen and contact the other colonies, nothing too special. She, as always, was the last one to arrive, and had to sit beside Cassie on the floor. Nate grinned from his spot in one of two seats.

"We're here to discuss the ice ceiling," John announced. He ignored Tabitha's groan.

"What about it, Cap?" Anthony asked.

“Sebastian has deemed the area safe to build support beams on and has requested that we begin constructing a support system for the ceiling.”

“Why do we need one?” Lucia asked. “We’re all safe in what we already have.”

“It’ll free up a lot of space,” Sebastian said. “We have extra protection from radiation and dust storms, we can work on making the space breathable—”

“With the technology we have right now, we won’t be able to fill the whole crater,” Tabitha reasoned. “At best, it’ll feel like extreme altitude sickness. At worst- well, we would die.”

“There have been reports of small asteroids colliding with Mars,” The Captain announced. “The NAMC and Korea Central have both announced that impacts have occurred just miles from their bases.”

“What’s ice gonna do against that?” Cassie wondered aloud.

“If the asteroid is large, not much- but with a thick ice cover, small collisions can be avoided. It’s an extra safety measure to keep us alive.”

Tabitha looked around at her crew. They were, dare she say it, friends, and close enough that she could read their expressions, though some were trying their best to keep their feelings under wraps. She knew that Seb was desperate to get this project on its feet. She could see that Nate was against it. When she looked at Cassie, she just saw distress. Tabitha sighed.

"There's a hell of a lot of cons to this, Seb," she began. He looked at her pleadingly.

"I know, but—"

"Let me finish. This ceiling will stop Nate from flying from Base, it will stop Lucia from studying the sky- but if we get hit, none of that will matter. I'd rather be inconvenienced than dead."

"Thank you, Tab," Seb smiled. She waved him off. She didn't do it for him.

Nate was glaring at her. She stared back at him calmly, until he looked away, to glare at someone else. Lucia giggled nearby.

"He's so mad at you," she whispered.

"What's he gonna do, fight me?" Tabitha replied. Nate huffed.

"He knows everyone listens to you."

"And so do I. You must be mad at me too."

"Why?"

"If this goes ahead, Seb will be fully invested. You'll be working alone."

"I know," Lucia sighed. "But it's not like he was fully focused when he was with me. I'm better off doing everything myself."

Tabitha snorted. Typical, she and Lucia were carrying more than their own weight. It was the sign of a strong woman to not rely on others, and Lucia had learned pretty quickly not to lean on Sebastian.

The Captain approved the Ice Ceiling. Nate stormed out of the room, followed by Cassie, and the others filed out after them until

only Tabitha and John were left.
“They’ll remember you supported this,” he told her quietly, and she nodded.
“I’ll never deny it. I stand by my word, whether it’s a good idea or not.”
“That’s a sign of a good leader,” he mused. Tabitha studied him for a moment. He’d aged the most visibly in their time on Mars. Everyone had started to look a little strange, getting paler and thinner and they all had the glassy eye syndrome. It was John that looked older. Tabitha had adjusted best to the New Martian Calendar, but even now she couldn’t quite figure out how age worked. Was John only two and-a-bit years older, or was he actually four years older? Either way, he’d gone completely grey, there were more creases on his face at the forehead, and the weight loss made him look frail and old. When she first met him, she thought that age suited him. Now she wasn’t so sure.

“Captain, what do you really think about this?” Tabitha asked. John sighed heavily.
“I think that it’s too ambitious, and only serves one purpose.”
“So why did you agree to it?”
“Because I see that everyone needs something to cling to,” he told her. “We all have something that keeps us sane here, and if I take that away from him, I don’t know what he would do.”
“I understand, Sir.”
“Tell me something now, Tabitha.”

"Of course, Sir."

"What do you cling to?"

Tabitha thought for a moment. What is it that kept her going on Mars? Was she simply better at adjusting? Was she just used to spending her time indoors, tinkering with equipment, and so it wasn't much different to her life back home? No, she decided eventually. Not anymore. She smiled.

"Sir, eventually another ship will come," she told him.

"Yes, the Agency has announced that their remaining funds will go on one final colony rocket."

"My sister works at the Agency, she has applied to board. Within a few years, she'll be here. That's what I cling to, Sir."

After sol down, the base went from work to play- at least, it did for those who stayed up late. Barely half of the colonists remained awake after a long sol of work, but Tabitha was one of the few who did, and she went straight to the food hall to find something fun to do.

"What's the game today, fellas?" She greeted, spotting a large group of people sitting around a table, a deck of cards spread out in front of them.

"I suggested poker," Sebastian said. "But apparently there's no chips to play."

"Of course there is," Tabitha snorted. "You can bet anything but money. Deal me in and let's see what's on offer."

The game became a strange mix of strip poker, truth or dare, and colonists trying to pawn off spare food and easy work. One man, who Tabitha thought was called Isaac, was telling anyone who would listen that he was trying to create alcohol in one of the farming domes and he'd bet his first bottle of beer on his hand.

"How are you making beer with no wheat?" Sebastian asked, amid titters. Isaac laughed.

"You can make beer out of anything if you're ambitious enough."

"I am not drinking anything with onions in it. Look at my face. I'm not kidding. If you bring me onion beer, I will drown you in it," Tabitha told him. Sebastian laughed.

"You heard her. Wheat or nothing. I'm all in."

Slowly, people folded, some went to bed, and Tabitha was left with a group of six men and women, with three players including her. She was confident with her cards; but she had no idea how to tell whether they were.

"Now, Tab; I'm going all in. My chips include Explorer."

The crowd 'oohed'. Sebastian had just won Explorer from a geologist, and Seb knew that Tabitha wanted it. The little Rover was her favourite piece of machinery, it needed an upgrade, and she'd been chasing it around the sectors like a mad woman to get her hands on it again.

"That's a pretty prize you're offering," she said. "And what might you want in return?"

"Your best builders for my project."

"I am not betting team Five on a card game," Tabitha snorted, "you can keep the robot."

"Tab, I'll get them one way or another, let's do this the fun way."

"If I win, you can't have them. No going to John, no requesting them. They're mine."

"All you gotta do is play."

It was stupid. She knew it was. But he'd only get them through the Captain anyway. At least this way she had a chance of winning something. She threw her cards down and hoped.

"Too bad, Seb," she grinned, pretending to scoop up imaginary poker chips. "I get the robot and the team. Sucks to lose, doesn't it?"

He didn't look happy. But he chose to gamble. Tabitha smiled to herself, and decided to call it a night. Best to quit whilst ahead, and Tabitha had Explorer. Anthony would no doubt come looking for her in the morning, enraged that one of his team lost her to a poker game, but hopefully he'd leave enough time for Tabitha to give her the software update she deserves.

He did appear the next morning, and waited whilst she worked on the Rover, thankfully allowing her the time she needed to do her work.

"I need to stop Georgie from gambling," he muttered under his breath, and Tabitha grinned.

"Hey, at least you're getting her back in good condition. I can't imagine how ratty she'd be if Sebastian had kept her- he knows nothing about caring for equipment."

"You're telling me. Has he come down here to collect more workers yet? I heard him discussing needing extra hands to work on his support system."

"He won't bother me," Tabitha laughed. "He's another fool who shouldn't gamble. He'd be an even bigger one if he thought he could go back on his bet."

Anthony snorted, and Tabitha declared Explorer free to go.

"You," he said, on his way out, "are a force to be reckoned with."

Tabitha already knew that much; but it was nice to hear it from someone else for a change. She smiled to herself and turned back to her projects, unconcerned with the ice ceiling that would be built far above her head. She had more important things to worry about.

6.
THE WORST MARSQUAKE
EARTH 2059///MARS 4A.C

LUCIA WAS LOSING HER MIND. Over three Martian years in, and she was no closer to figuring out Mars' magnetic field than she was when she arrived. Sebastian was no help; the man was obsessed with the ice ceiling, spending his days in charge of the Rovers and people assigned to putting it in place. So far, it was half-way done; the support structure was completely in place and C02 was being frozen over the top, the cold Martian winter allowing them to cool it quickly without using any power.

Maybe if he would help her with the problem he'd been sent here to solve, they wouldn't need ice at all.

"Why so far from your lab, Luc?" Anthony asked brightly. Anthony's geology lab had grown over the past Martian year, as his second tunnel had been dug through what he called 'a geologist's dream', whatever he meant by that. Any spare bodies had been brought in to study what he'd found, and Lucia was trying to be happy for him despite the bitterness she felt when she thought about her lack of progress. She leaned against an unused lab table, and sighed.

"I'm hitting wall after wall in my studies," she admitted, crossing her arms over her chest. She had paled in her time on Mars; she'd once had olive toned skin thanks to an Italian heritage, a summer glow that never faded, but Mars had taken it from her the way it took so many other things. She shouldn't be complaining about her skin, considering the rest of their problems, but it disappointed her every time she looked at her arms and saw how pale they'd become.

"What does Seb say?" Anthony asked, cradling what looked like a large chunk of rock in his arms as if it were a child. It was rather comical, how he handled it, but Lucia wasn't in the mood for jokes.

"He doesn't. His new job is the ice," she replied. Anthony sighed.

"So you want my help?"

"You're the only other person here who might have a clue about what's going on under our feet. Why Mars is… like this."

They'd all done their studies of Mars before they arrived, but everyone had their own interest; not many of the crew had studied plate tectonics, Mars' core and magnetic field.

"It's hard to say. I've been in contact with Tokyo and Iran, who have both reported minor Marsquakes in their area within the last few cycles or so."

"How minor is minor?" Lucia asked.

"Well, you know the Japanese and Earthquakes- it probably didn't register for them," he chuckled. "They were nothing to compare to an Earthquake- very low on the Richter scale."

"But it means there's plates, maybe a molten core," Lucia said, repeating what had been theorised for years. It felt like the next piece of information was right there in front of her, but she just couldn't see it. Like a word on the tip of her tongue, only it was in another language she couldn't yet understand. Anthony put down his large rock and patted her shoulder.

"Luc, I study rocks for a living. I can see them, touch them, and break them open. What you're trying to fathom out… Jeez, we hardly had it all figured out on Earth. Stop beating yourself up for not knowing how this planet ticks."

"But not knowing is keeping us indoors," Lucia replied. "Did Iran send you the data on their quake? Can I see it?"

"Of course. Hey, maybe if we get one, that might help you figure it out."

She'd laughed at the joke, not knowing what was coming. But then again, no one could predict the future. Lucia took the data and returned to her space, which was much quieter then Anthony's. Not many people wanted to dedicate themselves to something that seemed hopeless. At least she got some peace and quiet, away from pent up aggression and the glum mood that had spread across the base since Earth's last message.

The second colony ship, called Minerva, had carried 350 passengers. She held Britain's finest teachers, caregivers, Mothers and Fathers, handymen and jack of all traders. They were to build

New Kingdom's society, a way of life on Mars. The only problem was, they had never arrived. Minerva had launched in Britain at the same time a nuclear bomb had been dropped over Eastern Europe. Minerva was still in the atmosphere when the blast reached them, not quite quick enough to avoid the damage of the bomb. She'd gone down hard. According to the agency, there were no survivors, and the population of Britain had suffered badly from the effects of radiation, the whole island ordered to stay indoors. No one had come forward to claim the attack for their country. The minute of silence that New Kingdom had held when the news broke seemed too short, and rather useless. They were too far away to feel remembrance. Lucia finally accepted that she was a Martian, and that nobody else would be coming to join them.

"Do you spend every sol finding someone new to bother?" Tabitha greeted fondly, when Lucia entered her area. Tabitha had one of the biggest sectors, and she ran it so well that John never even had to assign roles or step in. Whilst Anthony's sector had been loud and slightly chaotic, Tabitha's space was running like a well-oiled machine, and Lucia had to take a moment to appreciate her leadership skills.

"I have no staff to pick on," Lucia replied easily, and Tabitha snorted.

"Well come here and make yourself useful, you've got small hands I could use."

Lucia knelt beside the machine that Tabitha was re-wiring. It looked like a back-up generator.

“What’s wrong with it?” She asked. Tabitha sighed.

“Some sort of power surge- Mars is wreaking havoc on my stuff. It’s either blowing a fuse or powering down, never in between.”

“That sucks.”

“Put your hand in there. I need you to pull a wire out for me.”

Lucia did not want to put her hand into what she now knew was a faulty machine, but Tabitha was giving her a stare that she couldn’t refuse, and so she reached inside, feeling for the wire in question.

“All the way out?”

“Not all the way. Gently, very gently, we don’t want to—” Lucia pulled, and the whole thing came out, a good few inches of wire completely disconnected from the machine. Tabitha huffed.

“That’s what we didn’t want to do.”

“I’m so sorry.”

“Its fine, hand it over. It looks a little worn out anyway.”

Lucia watched Tabitha examine the wire, before getting up to find a replacement. She was always so put together, always so confident. Sebastian had once joked that Tabitha was next in line to the Captain’s seat, but Lucia took it to heart; she couldn’t see anyone better to take over than Tab. Even when the news had broken about Minerva, she’d barely faltered, despite having family on board. Lucia wasn’t sure she could do the same, if it was her.

"I heard from Nate that our little Botanist is getting antsy," Tabitha said, nudging Lucia gently out of the way to get back to her work. Lucia made herself comfortable on the floor.

"When is she not? Cassie is always on the verge of a breakdown."

"It's worse now. Nate said that his request to fetch supplies from Beginnings was denied- again. He's asked several times in the past few years."

"Why would that hurt Cassie?" Lucia wondered. Tabitha shrugged.

"No idea but apparently, she's locked herself on the Calista and turned off her Comms."

"That's stupid," Lucia huffed. Calista hadn't been maintained since she landed, allowed to sit and rust and get damaged in the sun. Lucia rolled her eyes. Cassie had to be dramatic. It put them all at risk.

"She's too young to be here," Tabitha sighed. "Personality-wise. I see it on her. She wasn't ready to come to Mars. Now the poor girl is stuck here."

"Well that's not our fault," Lucia replied. "And her tantrum could hurt the rest of us. The ship isn't stable now it's being de-constructed, what was she thinking? One wrong move could finish the lot of us."

If Tabitha agreed, she didn't say anything. Lucia left her to her repairs, skulking around the base moodily. Cassie irritated her. So did Sebastian and his ice ceiling. So did the Captain for letting him go ahead with it. At this point, she could probably name several thousand reasons why her mood was sour.

Her initial reaction to the shudder was to think she was getting lightheaded; Europa had been conducting studies on how humans had adapted to the gravity alteration over a period of time, and found that many developed a sort of sickness from it, with one of the symptoms being dizziness and a slight difficulty with staying balanced. Lucia pressed her hand against the wall, trying to steady herself. When she felt the metal under her palm shaking, she felt a cold chill flood her chest.

Despite the strength workouts and the amount of time they'd spent on Mars, running was still a difficulty. Lucia's lungs burned and her muscles ached, still unable to adjust to Mars' gravitational pull. Lucia had hated running on Earth, but it was much worse here. Still, she pushed herself onward, hearing the sound of rumbling and screaming.

"Captain!" She yelled, when she reached his office.

"I know," he replied. "I've told everyone to gather in the food hall."

"Sir, where's Seb?"

"Outside, last I heard. The Comms have started to malfunction."

Lucia tried to turn hers on, but she heard a few crackling sounds, and then nothing. She tried again, pressing the button a little too hard. Nothing. She looked up at John.

"I can't reach him," she reported. John paled.

"When it stops, we can look for him, but I want no one leaving the base until it does. Do you understand? We need everyone to stay inside."

She nodded, and turned on her heel, heading for the food hall. She was hoping that he'd come in early, and she'd find him there, waving her concern away with a smile. Of course he'd be fine. Seb always was.

When Lucia arrived, she saw just over one hundred people, and none of them were Sebastian. She watched as they panicked, holding onto tables and walls as the ground shook beneath them. It was nothing that would even be deemed as major on Earth; but this had never happened to them here. Any natural disaster on Mars was likely to be worse.

"Lucia!" Anthony called, spotting her and making his way over. He looked like a new born deer, his balance all over the place. She held out her arms to steady him.

"I know you were joking," she said, "but please never wish for a Marsquake again."

He nodded stiffly.

"Where's Seb?" He asked.

"He was outside, I can't contact him. Comms have gone offline."

"I can't reach Hera," Nate announced, catching the attention of those around him. Despite the continuous shaking, everyone had gone silent.

"Why not?"

"I don't know."

"Is everyone here?" John demanded, arriving into the room with as much dignity as he could despite also struggling to stay upright.

"Everyone but Seb," Lucia said. The people around her began to nod, but Lucia caught sight of Nate. He had frozen in place, paling the way John had when he realised that Seb was in danger.

"Oh God," he breathed. "Cassie."

The sound from outside was rather like an explosion; Lucia instinctively threw herself to the floor at the noise, the sound of shattering, crumbling, rock being blasted apart on a grand scale. It made her head hurt. The screaming didn't help. It lasted for several long seconds, before everything went still and quiet, and heads began poking up from behind tables and chairs, raising from the floor a little. Lucia was half-way under Anthony, who had thrown himself over her as if to protect her. She met his eyes cautiously.

"What just happened?" He whispered.

"I have no idea. The quake has stopped."

John was the first to stand.

"Okay," he said, looking around at the crowd around him. "Who is going to help me look outside?"

7.
THE FIRST LOST THINGS
EARTH 2059///MARS 4A.C

ANTHONY HAD NEVER BEEN TO A FUNERAL. When his father passed, his Mother had left him with a babysitter, believing that little boys shouldn't have to watch their parents get buried. He always thought that it was a good thing, until now.

John hadn't spoken much in the past two weeks. The original crew had all spent the time in a sober silence, missing one of their own. When they joked about someone earning the title of first person to die in New Kingdom, they hadn't wanted it to be one of their friends. Anthony found support in his team; the geologists rallied around him when the base discovered what had happened after the quake, helped him start the investigation into why the ground collapsed. They had named the new feature in the crater 'The Pit'; about half a mile wide, it was a deep hole in the ground, black and seemingly endless. It had swallowed half of a farming dome, as well as the Calista II. The dome had been salvaged and swiftly placed over the top of The Pit, but the Calista was gone, disappeared somewhere in the depths of The Pit. That told Anthony that it was deeper than it seemed. The first time he'd seen

The Pit, he imagined it was about as deep as it was wide, but that definitely was not the case. The results of the tests they'd ran kept bringing up more questions.

"It's too deep for us to measure with the equipment we have," Nina reported, handing Anthony a tablet with the data they'd collected. He scanned the results on their tests, frowning. They couldn't measure the depth, how far it stretched under them, whether there was anything else down there worth looking at. He had no idea whether the ground they walked on was even safe, whether the quake had put them all in danger of disappearing downward if they moved too fast. The Captain wanted answers, as did everyone else, and Anthony was still receiving more questions.

"We need to make a report, give Cap something solid," Anthony muttered to himself. "We need to let the crew know what's happening."

He'd reached out to Tabitha, the first person he thought of in distress. She always seemed to know what to do and how to do it, and he was filled with relief when she came to help, weaving around the people in his sector to reach him.

"Talk to me," she greeted. Whilst others fell apart in the face of catastrophe, Tabitha hardened. Anthony sometimes missed her more playful side, but he was grateful for the strength she showed when he needed her.

"We don't have the answers that are needed right now," he

admitted. "We need more time, and more tests."

"Let's start with the most pressing issues, Anthony; you need to tell me, right now, if we are in imminent danger of the ground collapsing beneath us."

"Looking at how the ground gave way during the quake, I don't think we are; the area that sunk was a land site, Calista had hit it hard, and the rest of the crater held up during the quake, leading me to believe that it should be okay."

"Should be doesn't give me much confidence," Tabitha told him. "I believe your judgement, but you have to be sure."

"If it didn't collapse during the quake, we're fine- we just need to keep The Pit isolated and start working on stabilising the ground around it."

She nodded.

"I'll give you my teams, anything you need. Just make that thing safe, okay?"

Anthony started delegating tasks to his sector, splitting them into groups to tackle The Pit. He had people on coming up with supports, others on figuring out what was inside, a few on analysing samples. He also had a small number of people set on trying to contact Calista. The comms they had were still down, but the ship could still receive signals through different means, and if there was any chance that the ship had survived the fall, they had to know. Anthony had to be certain that he wasn't leaving Cassie alone down there if she was alive. If she was, they could find a way to pull her back to the surface, and he wouldn't have to attend his first funeral.

Nate was taking it the hardest. Anthony had heard from a few workers that his sector was at a standstill, with no one to lead them. He spent his days outside, wandering in a wide circle around The Pit, talking to no one. Anthony had tried to talk to him, they all had, but Nate was uncharacteristically quiet, and Anthony didn't know what to do with that. He just got on with his job and hoped that Emily could get through to him.

"Anthony, do you have a report for me?" John asked. He wasn't often seen in Anthony's neck of the woods, but the lack of comms had meant that everyone had to walk further to get their messages across. A few spare hands had volunteered to serve as a sort of messenger system, running messages and requests back and forth, but it was unorganised and hard to track, and Anthony had found that there was never anyone around when he needed them. It would seem that John felt the same, judging by his visit.

"I do, Sir, but you won't like it," Anthony replied, handing John an updated set of results on his tablet. John scanned the screen and sighed.

"Is there no sign of Calista?" He asked quietly. Anthony shuffled uncomfortably.

"No, Sir. The Pit is… so much deeper than we know, even a big ship is swallowed by it. We keep trying to contact her, but…"

Anthony knew that John was a widow, and he had no children of his own; he had seen how his Captain had behaved around Cassie, treating her differently from the others, as if she was a child he needed to care for. Sometimes, Anthony thought he was too strict on her, but he hadn't brought it up. It seemed a little late to mention it now, so he kept his mouth shut.

"It's okay, Anthony. This is not an ideal situation," John sighed.

Anthony bit his lip, debating on whether to ask or not.

"Sir," he began, deciding to despite his better judgment. "Do we know why the comms are down yet?"

"We do," John replied heavily. It wasn't good news.

"Oh. Its… it's not the dust storm, is it?"

The storm had rolled in just a few hours after the quake, like Mars hadn't already damaged them enough. Martian dust storms were fierce, they were dangerous, and they lasted for months. The second the wind picked up, Anthony knew that Hera would have trouble keeping everyone connected, but complete radio silence was odd.

"It isn't. But we shouldn't speculate when we don't have all the details. I'm hoping that it's a problem that will be fixed quickly."

Anthony knew better than to hope. He'd hoped for Lucia that she would have a Marsquake to study, and now there was a gaping hole in their back yard and Cassie was gone. Sebastian, who had been outside at the time, had just managed to escape with his life; he had seen the ship go down first hand, and nearly went with it-when he'd reached the safety of inside, he hadn't spoken for several hours, in too much shock to get the words out. Anthony still wasn't sure whether he'd recovered, as every time he looked at Seb, he saw a haunted look on his face that made him feel cold and uncomfortable.

At sol down, Anthony made his way to John's office. The sol had been long and too quiet, his meal was bland and sat uncomfortably in his stomach, and Anthony wanted nothing more than to lie in the dark and pretend that he was back home on Earth, in his grandmother's house. She would always be playing music in the evening, something from the days of her youth, and Anthony could fall asleep listening to the sound of better days. Most of the original crew were already inside John's office, bar Lucia and Seb, who were probably on their way. The space on the floor that Cassie usually filled was depressingly empty. Anthony took one of the chairs and stared at the wall, ignoring the obvious absence.

When everyone arrived, John began their meeting.

"It's been two weeks," he said, looking at each of them in turn. "It's time we face the truth. Humans cannot survive that long without sustenance. If the fall didn't kill her, it's safe to say that Cassandra…is dead."

He croaked out the last word, and Nate flinched at the sound, shaking his head. Lucia and Seb sat side by side, her hand on his arm. Tabitha was a blank slate, eyes fixed on John carefully.

"We should… do something for her. A memorial, of sorts," Lucia suggested. “To say goodbye.”

Nate made a noise that Seb glared at.

“What’s your problem?” He asked darkly. Nate looked up at him. He’d been crying.

“You all care so much now,” he spat. “Where were you the past year, when she was struggling?”

“Nate,” John warned. Nate let out a forceful laugh.

“You,” he said. “You were the worst- acting like you cared, but everything you did was another nail in the coffin- all she wanted was her samples, you couldn’t give her that? You let him build a god damn ceiling over our heads for no reason, but you wouldn’t—”

“Don’t talk to me like that,” John ordered.

“You talked to her like she was a child! You all treated her like dirt! And now it’s all fine and you can pretend it’s not your fault she was in that damn ship in the first place. Well I’m not gonna disrespect her like that. She’s dead, and you’re the reason.”

He looked at all of them, even Anthony, who felt his meal fighting to get back out of his mouth. Lucia looked like she’d been slapped. Anthony found that his eyes went downward, right to the space that wasn’t filled.

“Nate,” Tabitha said eventually. “You’re right.”

“Excuse me?” Seb demanded.

“Captain, Nate and I will be borrowing a Rover,” Tabitha said. It wasn’t a request.

"And where will you go?" John asked. Tabitha and Nate exchanged a look.

"We're getting what Cassie asked for years ago. Come on, Nate. We'll grab Emily on the way, the three of us will get her samples." Nate nodded, satisfied, though Anthony thought he heard him mutter something about it being 'too little, too late'. John let them go, sighing heavily and slumping in his seat. Anthony said nothing. He didn't think he could think of the right words to say.

Anthony's first ever funeral was nothing like he'd imagined. Firstly, because it was on a different planet. Secondly, because the hole in the ground was half a mile wide, and third, because the body was already down there. They all wore space suits, the five of them that were in attendance. Everyone else was inside, holding a few minutes of silence in respect for Cassie. Anthony watched as Nate knelt in the sand, opening a small sealed bag and placing its contents on the ground. It was moss, samples from Earth that Cassie had requested when Beginnings had announced its trip. All she had wanted was moss. Had it been so hard to give it to her?

"It won't grow," Lucia said, once they'd returned inside. They sat together in the food hall, everyone but John, all slumped and gloomy. Emily had joined them, hand in hand with Nate.

"Cassie would've found a way," Nate replied. Anthony swallowed.

"She did have a talent with plants. She managed to keep us all fed for four years."

"Let's hope she passed on her skills to someone else."

John's sudden arrival had everyone looking up in alarm. He was in a hurry, and his expression made Anthony nervous. They exchanged worried glances.

"Where's the fire, Cap?" Tabitha asked. John looked at them all for a moment, expression grim. He looked at them like he was preparing himself for the worst.

"Captain?" Seb prompted.

"Hera M-14 is gone," he said eventually, receiving gasps and looks of shock from his crew.

"What?"

"The Satellite is gone, likely crash landed on Mars somewhere. Its bad timing, considering, but we need to buckle up."

"You're scaring me," Lucia admitted. "What does that mean?"

"That means our safety net is gone. We can't contact Earth," Tabitha guessed. John nodded.

"Get ready, everyone. From here on in, we're on our own."

The crew exchanged looks, some scared, some determined. Anthony closed his eyes for a moment, trying to find some composure. He would need it now. He took a deep breath, before opening them again.

"I guess then," he said, catching the attention of his peers. "That it's time to get to work."

It wouldn't be easy, not a single moment of it. But humans had a knack for surviving, even in the harshest conditions. Anthony had faith that, even without the help from Earth, that they could make Mars their own, and they would thrive here the way they had back home. If they couldn't- well, he didn't want to think of that. Best to remain optimistic.

Around The Pit edge, the moss remained, green and healthy, and slowly, very slowly, it would begin to grow.

45335519R00045

Printed in Poland
by Amazon Fulfillment
Poland Sp. z o.o., Wrocław